Daniel Visits the Doctor

adapted by Becky Friedman
based on the screenplay written by Andrea Maywhort and Eric Saiet
poses and layouts by Jason Fruchter

Simon Spotlight
New York   London   Toronto   Sydney   New Delhi

SIMON SPOTLIGHT
An imprint of Simon & Schuster Children's Publishing Division
1230 Avenue of the Americas, New York, New York 10020
First Simon Spotlight edition August 2014
© 2014 The Fred Rogers Company
For information about special discounts for bulk purchases, please contact Simon & Schuster
Special Sales at 1-866-506-1949 or business@simonandschuster.com.
Manufactured in the United States of America 0714 LAK
10 9 8 7 6 5 4 3 2 1
ISBN 978-1-4814-1734-1
ISBN 978-1-4814-1735-8 (eBook)

It was a beautiful day in the neighborhood, and Daniel was home, playing doctor.

"Okay, Tigey, it's time for Doctor Daniel to give you a checkup."
Daniel giggled as he opened his toy doctor kit. Just then Mom Tiger
came into the room.

"Oh hello, Doctor, have you seen my little tiger, Daniel?" Mom asked.

"Mom, it's me . . . Daniel! I'm not really a doctor!" Daniel giggled.

Mom smiled and ruffled Daniel's fur. "Well, Daniel, time to stop
playing because we have to get going," Mom said.

"Where are we going?" asked Daniel.

"We're going to see Dr. Anna today," said Mom. "It's time for your checkup."

"But . . . Mom, I'm one stripe scared to go for a checkup," said Daniel. "What will happen there?"

Mom put her arm around Daniel and sang, *"When we do something new, let's talk about what we'll do."*

Mom showed Daniel what would happen at the doctor's office and started to draw. The first thing that happens at the doctor is that you wait . . . in the waiting room. Daniel remembered that Dr. Anna's waiting room had a fish tank, books, and toys, too!

The next thing that happens is that Dr. Anna will check your body to make sure it's healthy and strong. She'll check your heart—*thump, thump!* She'll check your ears—*tickle, tickle, tickle*—she'll check your eyes—*blink, blink*—and she'll check your throat—*aaaaaah!*

"Will I have to get a shot?" Daniel asked Mom. Mom shook her head no. Not today.

Daniel took Mom's pictures to Dr. Anna's with him. "It's like a book!" said Daniel, as they headed out the door.

"It is like a book!" said Mom Tiger. "Let's see if you can find all the things we drew in our book . . . in Dr. Anna's office!"

"Okay!" said Daniel.

"It's time for a checkup, so we're off to the doctor's office, won't you ride along with me?" sang Daniel and Mom Tiger, as Trolley rolled toward Dr. Anna's office.

"Wow!" said Daniel, as he looked around Dr. Anna's office. "The waiting room looks just like the picture we drew!" Daniel ran over to the fish tank. "Hi, fishies! *Blub, blub, blub!*"

"And now," said Mom, "we wait. *Wait, wait, wait in the waiting room.*"

While he was waiting in the waiting room, Daniel made-believe that the fish in the fish tank were going to see the doctor too!

"Daniel Tiger, and . . . Tigey Tiger," called Dr. Anna.
"It is time for your checkups. Follow me!"
Mom held Daniel's hand as they followed Dr. Anna.

Daniel climbed up on the table and looked around curiously. What was going to happen next?

Dr. Anna smiled and sang to Daniel, *"When we do something new, let's talk about what we'll do."*

First Dr. Anna listened to Tigey's heartbeat with a stethoscope. *"Thump, thump!"* Dr. Anna said with a smile.

Then Dr. Anna listened to Daniel's heartbeat. *Thump, thump!* "Your heart is strong and healthy, Daniel!" said Dr. Anna.

Dr. Anna even let Daniel listen to his own heart with the stethoscope! *Thump, thump!* Daniel thought that was so cool!

Dr. Anna used her otoscope to check Tigey's ears. *"Tickle, tickle, tickle!"* Dr. Anna said.

Then Dr. Anna checked Daniel's ears. *Tickle, tickle, tickle!* "The otoscope does tickle!" Daniel giggled.

Dr. Anna checked Daniel's eyes. *Blink, blink!*

And then she checked Daniel's throat. *Aaaaaah!*

Dr. Anna checked Tigey's height and weight. Tigey was a healthy weight and three stripes tall!

Then she checked Daniel's height and weight. Daniel was a healthy weight and eight stripes tall. "That's the perfect number of stripes for a tiger your age!" Dr. Anna said.

"Daniel and Tigey, you are both done with your checkups," said Dr. Anna, "and you both get a heart sticker for being such good patients."

"Grr-ific! Thanks, Dr. Anna!" said Daniel.

Back in the waiting room, Daniel saw his friend O the Owl.

"Hello, Daniel! I'm here for my checkup," said O the Owl, looking nervous.

"You are?" asked Daniel. "I just had my checkup!"

"What was it like?" asked O the Owl.

"You can read this book I made with my mom," said Daniel, handing O the book. "It will tell you all about it."

"A book?" said O the Owl happily. "I love books! Thanks, Daniel!"

Daniel and Mom Tiger walked out of Dr. Anna's office. Trolley was waiting for them.

"Hi, Trolley!" said Daniel. "Guess what? I'm nice and healthy! And so is Tigey."

"Ding, ding!" said Trolley, and then took Daniel and Mom Tiger all the way home.

Thanks for coming with me and Tigey to the doctor's office. Did you find all the things I drew in my book in Dr. Anna's office? Knowing what was going to happen helped me feel good about going to the doctor. And it might help you feel good too! Ugga Mugga.

Are you getting ready to go to the doctor's office? Maybe your doctor's office will have some of the same things as Dr. Anna's! Take this book with you when you go to the doctor. How many of these things does your doctor have?

exam table

scale

books

stethoscope

magazines

height chart

fish tank

otoscope

toys

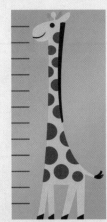